Lucy
and the
Magic
Crystal

Other titles in this series

Lucy
and the
Magic
Crystal

gillian shields

illustrated by helen turner

BLOOMSBURY
CHILDREN'S
BOOKS

Map of

Coral Kingdom

Cauldron Cliff

Oceania

Giant Kelp Forest

Rocky Islands

Fishing Nets

Shipwreck

First published in Great Britain in 2006 by Bloomsbury Publishing Plc,
36 Soho Square, London, W1D 3QY

Text copyright © 2006 by Gillian Shields
Illustrations copyright © 2006 by Helen Turner

A CIP catalogue record of this book is available from the British
Library

ISBN 0 7475 8770 1
ISBN-13 9780747587705

Printed and bound in Great Britain by Clays Ltd, St Ives Plc

1 3 5 7 9 10 8 6 4 2

All papers used by Bloomsbury Publishing are natural, recyclable
products made from wood grown in well-managed forests. The manufacturing
processes conform to the environmental regulations of the country of origin.

For Sarah - my best friend and
queen of the eco-warriors
- *G.S.*

In memory of my irreplaceable friend
Jeanette, who had such a sense of fun,
style and laughter. I was lucky to
have known her.
- *H.T.*

Prologue

Meet Misty, Ellie, Sophie, Holly, Lucy and Scarlett. They are mermaid Sisters of the Sea, who live in the magical underwater world of Coral Kingdom. The Merfolk and their wise ruler, Queen Neptuna, look after the sea and all its creatures.

Coral Kingdom is protected by six powerful magic Crystals, which give life and strength to the Merfolk.

Without the Crystals, Coral Kingdom would not survive.

Every year, the old Crystals fade and have to be replaced. Queen Neptuna sends Misty and her friends – six special mermaids who are pure of heart - to fetch the new ones from the secret Crystal Cave. But as they are bringing the Crystals home, a storm blows the mermaids completely off course.

This is no ordinary storm! It is created by Mantora, Queen

Neptuna's jealous sister. Mantora wanted to rule Coral Kingdom, and now she is bitter and full of hatred. She is determined to stop the mermaids reaching home, so that she can overthrow Queen Neptuna and set up her evil Storm Kingdom instead.

Luckily, the young mermaids have courage and friendship on their side. But that's not all; their SOS Kits will help them as they race to get the Crystals back safely. And they never forget their Mermaid Pledge:

We promise that we'll take good care
Of all sea creatures everywhere.
We'll never hurt and never break,
We'll always give and never take.
And as we fight Mantora's threat,
This saying we must not forget:
'I'll help you and you'll help me,
For we are Sisters Of the Sea!'

Misty and her friends are eager to prove that Queen Neptuna was right to trust them with the precious Crystals. They are going to do everything it takes to get them home and safeguard Coral Kingdom for another year.

Will Mantora win? Or can the mermaids get the new Crystals back in time to stop the light fading for ever from Coral Kingdom?

Lucy

Chapter One

Lucy was working hard to keep up with the other mermaids – Misty, Ellie, Sophie, Holly, and Scarlett – as they swam past Sandy Bay Island in the dawn's early light. They darted through the waves like bright sea nymphs, eagerly swishing their sparkling tails in a desperate race against time. Coral Kingdom lay hidden under the waves in the West, and the young friends had to get the magic Crystals home before sunset, or the power of the Merfolk would fade for ever.

The shy young mermaid with the pearly green tail was feeling anxious. What if she couldn't swim as fast as the others, Lucy fretted. If only she was strong and swift, like Sophie and Scarlett! Lucy tried to push herself harder, as the mermaids headed out to sea. They wanted to be far from the shore before any early morning fishing boats set off from the Island.

'I must get home in time,' she thought. 'I can't let everyone down.' Lucy felt the precious Crystal, which she was carrying in her green pouch, bump against her waist. She hoped that its magic would give her strength and courage. Trying to imagine the Crystal's glittering radiance, Lucy surged after her friends.

But just at that moment, a large black bird with a grey bill and yellow chin wheeled above them. It was a splendid cormorant.

'Stop, Sisters of the Sea,' he cried.

Lucy looked up worriedly. 'You're friends with the sea birds,' she whispered to Ellie, who was near her. 'Explain to him that we can't stop, not for anything.'

'We cannot stay, my friend,' Ellie called up to him. 'Queen Neptuna is waiting for us.'

'And Mantora is waiting for you!' he replied.

The mermaids stopped swimming and looked at each other in horror. Then the cormorant settled on the waves in front of them, as they bobbed up and down.

'What do you mean? Have you seen Mantora?' they all asked him at once.

'I have indeed,' said the bird with a sigh. 'My name is Chad. Late last night, I was flying home over the sea between here and Coral Kingdom. I spotted a strange, dark shape, lurking in the water. It was Mantora, but she wasn't alone.'

'Who was with her?' faltered Lucy.

The cormorant lowered his voice. 'She has summoned her sea serpents from the depths of the ocean. They are like dragon-headed snakes, with cold green eyes and gaping mouths. Troops of stinging jellyfish are at her side. And in the air, her dark Storm Gulls are gathering. Mantora is lying in wait for you – with an army!'

'What can we do?' shuddered Misty.

'However will we get past them?'

'You will not be able to,' replied Chad. 'There are too many of them.'

'But…but, we can't just give up,' said Lucy shyly. 'Not after all we've been through to get this far.'

The bird turned his head to look at her with his kind, clear eyes. 'Mantora may be too strong for six young mermaids,' he said, 'but you have many friends. The Lord Albatross has sent swift messengers to every corner of the wide sea, telling all the creatures of your great deeds. Now you must raise an army of your own, to defend the Crystals.'

The mermaids looked shocked. 'An army! But how…where…who shall we ask?'

'My brothers are at your service for a start,' Chad smiled. He lifted himself from the water and flapped his great wings. A host of cormorants came streaming down on the morning breeze, like black arrows. They landed on the sea in a shower of silver droplets.

'We will match Mantora's Storm Gulls,

beak for beak, and wing for wing,' they
declared.

'Thank you so much,' said the
mermaids. This seemed like a good
beginning.

'But how will we fight her jellyfish?'
wondered Ellie.

'I've got an idea about that,' said Holly
quickly. 'Jellyfish are poisonous. So we
need to find some of the friendly fish, who
use stings to protect themselves, and ask if
they will join us.'

'That's brilliant, Holly,' said Sophie.
'Perhaps some of the scorpion fish will
help.'

'And some lion fish, too,' added Scarlett.
'They are fierce fighters when they have to
be. Come on, Sophie, let's go and look for

them on the reefs.'

The two friends plunged swiftly under the waves, calling out, 'We'll be back soon!'

'Now we need a plan for dealing with Mantora's sea serpents,' said Holly, looking very serious. 'But which creatures are big and brave enough to stand up to those monsters?'

The clever young mermaid held her head in her hands and tried to think. Misty and Ellie frowned with concentration, rippling their gleaming tails gently in the water.

Lucy looked down in despair. She was secretly very frightened at the idea of a real battle, and was sure that she wouldn't be able to come up with any good ideas. But then she gasped. Several huge, silent shapes were floating beneath her, making their way menacingly along the deep sea bed.

'I've just thought of something,' Lucy blurted out, looking up at the others.

'What?' asked Holly.

'Sharks!'

Chapter Two

'Sharks?' said Ellie, in a worried voice. 'Do we really want to get mixed up with sharks?'

'Not all of them are mean, Ellie,' said Lucy.

'But how can we find any?' asked Holly. 'The sun is already up and time is rushing on. We can't just stay here hoping that some will swim by. We have to do something.'

'Well, why don't we ask those sharks down there to help us?' replied Lucy timidly. 'They look big enough to scare anybody.'

The mermaids peered down through the blue waves. They saw the majestic outline of some huge fish, slowly swaying along in the deep water below them. These weren't just ordinary sharks; they were Whale Sharks, some of the largest and most impressive creatures in the whole Ocean.

'They would be perfect to frighten off Mantora's sea serpents, Lucy,' exclaimed Holly. 'How clever of you.'

Lucy blushed with pleasure.

'Let's go and talk to them,' said Misty eagerly. She flicked her pink tail and dived

under the water. Holly followed, but Ellie hesitated.

'Are you sure they're safe, Lucy?' she murmured. 'They look awfully big.'

'Whale Sharks are gentle giants really,' replied Lucy. 'Don't worry, they won't bite.'

She dived down, with Ellie following cautiously behind. The sharks looked even more powerful when the mermaids came near them. They had immensely long brown bodies, dotted over with white markings. Their smooth, flat heads ended in gigantic, grinning mouths. But Lucy, who was often nervous about all sorts of things, was not in the least bit frightened. The vast sharks seemed to give her courage as they glided silently through the ocean.

'Don't go any further!' she called to them. 'We desperately need your help. A dangerous enemy is lurking in wait for us. And she's your enemy, too!'

The biggest Whale Shark slowly turned his great head to look at her.

'An enemy?' he said. 'What enemy does Yerik the chief shark need to fear?' His mouth opened wide as he spoke, displaying row after row of pointed teeth.

'One who wants to destroy the power of Queen Neptuna, and harm the sea and all its creatures,' said Lucy impressively. Then the sharks gathered in a large circle around her. They listened carefully as she explained about the Crystals and Mantora's evil troops, lying in wait ahead.

'So now we need an army, too,' Lucy said. 'It will be the army of Queen Neptuna, defending all the rightful creatures of the Ocean against Mantora.'

'We do not fear Mantora,' boomed Yerik, 'or her sea serpents. But we are afraid of what will happen to our seas if her Storm Kingdom is triumphant.'

The sharks spoke to each other in their deep voices, whilst the mermaids waited anxiously.

'Very well,' said Yerik, at last. 'We will join your army. And we will frighten that miserable Mantora and her wretched sea serpents so much that they will never return to these waters again!'

All the sharks laughed, opening up their enormous mouths.

'Ha, ha, ha!' they rumbled. They did look rather alarming. But Lucy was so grateful to them that she threw her arms round Yerik's nose and kissed him.

'Thank you so much,' gulped Ellie.

Then Lucy noticed Sophie and Scarlett hovering in the clear water, at a little distance from the sharks.

'It's all right,' she cried, waving her arms quickly. 'Yerik and his people are our friends. They're going to help us beat Mantora.'

'Thank goodness,' said Scarlett, with a sigh of relief.

She and Sophie glided gracefully over to the others. A shoal of strange-looking creatures followed them. Brightly striped lion fish, with billowing orange fronds like a mane, swam behind Sophie.

Grim-looking scorpion fish, bright red and bristling with sharp spikes, formed a determined rank of soldiers behind Scarlett.

'We can sting Mantora's jellyfish,' they shouted. 'We're not afraid of her.'

Lucy's heart began to thump. She hoped none of these brave creatures would be hurt by Mantora.

'Now we must go and tell Chad, the captain of the cormorants, that our army is ready,' declared Holly. The mermaids looked at each other apprehensively. They had never expected this. Queen Neptuna's army was on the move!

Chapter Three

It was past midday and the sky was grey
and threatening. In the distance, a
menacing crowd of ragged gulls swooped
and swirled on the wind. The mermaids
had reached the far Western Waves.

'We are nearly there,' said the
cormorant gravely, hovering over the
young friends. 'Mantora's storm clouds are
gathering ahead. Beyond her, Coral

Kingdom is waiting for you. This will be the battle ground.'

Battle! Lucy's heart fluttered and she felt rather sick. She wasn't sure whether she was brave enough to face it. What if a jellyfish stung her? How would she keep hold of her Crystal in all the noise and confusion?

As though he had read her thoughts, Chad said, 'You must stay well back when the fighting starts, Sisters of the Sea.'

'No!' Lucy exclaimed. She swallowed hard and steeled herself to be strong. 'However scary it is, we're going to face this with you and Yerik and the others. We're all in this together as a team.'

'Of course we are,' said Misty. The others nodded solemnly in agreement.

'Very well,' replied the bird. 'Let us fight
for Queen Neptuna and all free folk of the
sea.'

Then Chad and the cormorants flew like
black rain in the direction of Mantora's
Storm Gulls. The shadowy, underwater
shapes of the sharks and fish raced along
beneath the great birds to meet their foe.
With a rainbow flash of their jewelled

tails, the mermaids leapt through the clear waters, speeding on and on. Queen Neptuna's army was sweeping bravely into battle, chanting their valiant cry:

We do not fear Mantora,
Hidden in her deep sea lair;
For Queen Neptuna's army
Is advancing – so beware!

As the courageous friends charged forward, the rumour and noise of their advance spread through the sea. Other creatures came to join them; lobsters, manta rays, dolphins, turtles and countless small fish, all eager to help. Soon, the mermaids were surrounded by a great throng of brave and loyal friends.

'We'll fight with you,' they cried. 'We're tired of Mantora spoiling everything.'

Lucy's heart swelled with gratitude, as she swam through the sparkling waves. The support of all these faithful creatures would give her the courage to face the task ahead. But before she had time to think, Chad called out in a ringing voice, 'The time has come. Let battle commence!'

Looking up quickly, Lucy saw Chad and his brothers charging to attack Mantora's cunning birds. But the Storm Gulls put up a fierce resistance; pecking, darting, wheeling and scratching the brave cormorants. Then a terrible sight rose from the sea, in front of the mermaids.

Mantora burst above the waves, looking like no other mermaid that Lucy and her friends had ever seen before. She was dressed in a fearsome breastplate that gleamed dully like armour, and her strong arms were bound with heavy, clanking bracelets. In her hand she held a sharp spear, with a dangerous net hanging from it. Her hair was midnight black, and her face – but then Lucy gasped. They couldn't see her face! The malignant mermaid wore a long ragged veil, held in place by a glinting, spiky crown. The veil concealed her features, but Lucy glimpsed two red eyes, flashing with hatred.

Raising her spear, Mantora shrieked, 'Powers of the Dark Storm, arise!'

The sky suddenly grew black, and bolts

of lightning flashed near the mermaids. Beneath them, the angry sea seethed and leapt. Dark shapes thrashed in the water, and snaky green tentacles writhed above the waves.

Lucy feverishly took out her Crystal and clutched it close to her heart. 'Give us strength and courage!' she whispered.

'Get under the water, away from the lightning,' Holly shouted. Lucy and the others plunged into the sea. There was a confused swirl, as the hideous sea serpents attacked on all sides, lashing out against the brave turtles and lion fish and scorpion fish ranged against them. Shouts and cries and the sounds of bitter struggles echoed though the churning water.

Then the terrifying figure of Mantora sank under the waves, surrounded by transparent jellyfish, which surged towards the young mermaids.

'The Crystals!' yelled Sophie. Soon they were all holding up their Crystals as

precious weapons in this desperate fight
against their enemy.

'*Mermaid SOS!*' they cried bravely. At
that instant, strange blue rays of light,
like freezing ice, shot from the Crystals.

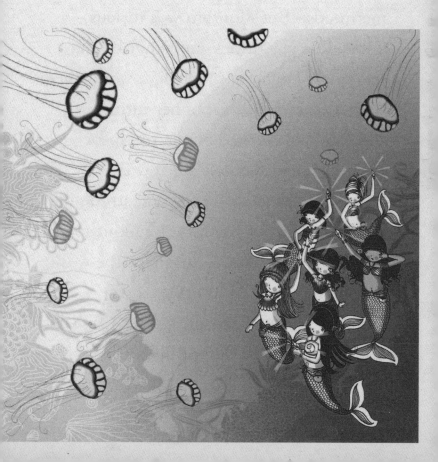

These cold, piercing beams stung Mantora's jellyfish again and again, until the poisonous creatures fell helplessly down into the depths, as the great battle raged on all sides.

'Oh, well done, everyone,' exclaimed the mermaids. But Mantora was furious. 'How dare you attack my jellyfish,' she screamed. Lurching suddenly towards them with a powerful thrust of her tarnished tail, Mantora flicked her netted spear towards Lucy. Wooosh! Lucy was immediately caught in the net, struggling to find a way out from its close-knit ropes. Her heart was beating wildly as she was dragged towards Mantora's terrible clutches. She tried to hold up her Crystal, but her arms were pinned by her sides.

'Now you will truly learn to fear me,'
Mantora hissed, as she got ready to snatch
Lucy. But at that moment a tremendous
bellow rang out above the noise of the
battle.

'WE…DO…NOT…FEAR…MANTORA!'

It was Yerik and his huge sharks. They burst up from the deep waters, their wide mouths spread in grim smiles which displayed their glittering teeth. Yerik propelled himself near to Lucy, still trapped at the end of Mantora's spear. With one swift movement, he ripped the net to shreds and Lucy wriggled free.

'Swim away, little ones,' he boomed. 'Leave us to deal with this traitor!'

As Lucy sped up to the surface with the others, she caught a glimpse of a haggard face beneath Mantora's veil. Her dark eyes glowed with fear, as she was surrounded by the giant sharks. Mantora gave a strangled yell, and tried to hold her spear aloft. Yerik smashed it into smithereens with a single blow from his powerful tail.

'Noooo!' she howled. The last thing the
mermaids saw was a frantic swirl as
Mantora tried to plunge away in a
desperate attempt to escape.

Above the sea, feathers drifted down
from the sky like dark snow. Lucy could

see that the cormorants were still fighting bravely in the howling wind. The rain whipped through the air and glassy green waves rose up like sheer cliffs around the young friends. Suddenly, a small battered boat rode precariously over the top of one of the waves, and dashed down the other side. A terrified Human face peeped over the edge of the boat. Someone had been caught up in Mantora's battle storm!

Chapter Four

'Why, that's John Robert's boat,' gasped
Scarlett. 'But that's not John in it.'

The mermaids looked up as the faded
green boat spun round in front of them. A
pale young face stared pleadingly into
Lucy's eyes over its side, looking sick with
fear.

'He's only a boy,' said Lucy. 'It must be
John's son – Jack!'

At that moment, the wind suddenly dropped and Holly cried out, 'Look, the Storm Gulls are flying away.'

It was true. Mantora's crow-like birds were fleeing from the site of the battle. They darted wildly here and there, trying to escape from Chad and his brothers, who were chasing them into the distance. The waves died down again, the sun broke through the clouds, and its golden rays shone once more on to a calm blue sea. Under the water, the serpents sank out of sight, and Mantora was nowhere to be seen.

'Mantora's army has been defeated!' cheered the mermaids. They burst out singing for joy:

Our friends are safe,
The battle's done,
Listen to our victory song!
Our way is clear,
Mantora's gone,
Listen to our thankful song!
We'll reach our home
Before too long,
Listen to our joyful song!

As they sang, the look on the boy's face changed from fear to delight.

'I knew it,' he breathed. 'I knew Dad was right all the time. There really are mermaids!'

'Yes,' said Scarlett severely, 'and there really are little boys who take boats which don't belong to them. What are you doing in John's boat?'

'John Roberts is my dad,' said the boy proudly. 'And you must be Scarlett. You're the one Dad caught, aren't you?' He looked around at the friends as they bobbed up and down in the water near his storm-scarred boat. 'The kind-looking mermaid with the red hair must be Lucy,' he added. 'Dad told me all your names.'

'He told you our names?' spluttered Sophie. 'But we put a Forgetting Charm on him so that he wouldn't remember seeing us!'

'I reckon you didn't make it strong enough for him,' grinned Jack. 'Anyway, last night, he came into my room to tell me a bedtime story. He said he'd had a strange dream about the Merfolk. He told me all about taking you to Cauldron Cliff. Then he said, "But mind son, it was only a dream." '

'We should have made that Forgetting Charm much stronger,' muttered Holly under her breath.

'I wanted it so much to be true,' Jack carried on, 'that I couldn't sleep at all. So I crept out of our cottage on Sandy Bay Island this morning, before anyone had woken up. I took Dad's boat and rowed out West to look for you. That's where he said the kingdom of the Merfolk lay hidden. And I'm so glad I did.'

His face shone as he looked at Lucy and her friends.

'Dad thinks I'm going to be a fisherman when I grow up, but I'm not. I'm going to be an underwater explorer, to find out all about the sea and protect it.' Then he remembered something and his sunny smile dimmed. 'Dad will be so worried, though. The boat was damaged in that strange storm which blew up from nowhere, and I've lost the oars overboard. I don't know how I'm going to get back!'

Lucy thought about John, anxiously waiting for his boy at home. It made her think longingly about her own parents, worrying over her in Coral Kingdom.

'We'll try and get you home,' she said softly. 'Somehow…'

'I don't think we can, Lucy,' interrupted Scarlett. 'We can't waste any time rescuing Humans just now.'

'Don't be too hard on him, Scarlett,' pleaded Lucy. 'He only came out here to see the Merfolk, after all.'

'It is sort of our fault, in a way,' added Misty. 'If we had put a better Forgetting Charm on John, this might not have happened.'

'But what can we do?' asked Sophie, swishing her tail impatiently. 'We must swim straight on. The battle is over and the sunset is only a few hours away.'

'You see, Jack,' said Lucy, swimming closer to him, 'we're on an urgent mission for Queen Neptuna. Look!'

She shyly showed her Crystal to the eager young boy. The sun's

rays reflected from it, like sparks of fire.

Wonderingly, Jack held out his sunburnt hand over the

edge of the boat. Lucy carefully lowered the Crystal into his outstretched palm, where it seemed to shine brighter than ever. The other mermaids watched in surprise.

'Can you feel the strong young magic in it, Jack?' Lucy whispered solemnly. 'We must get the Crystals to Coral Kingdom before sunset, or the power of the Merfolk will fade for ever.'

'Then go at once,' Jack cried, giving the precious Crystal back to her. 'Leave me here, I don't mind. I'll get home somehow. You can't let your powers die because of me!'

Then the mermaids heard the beating of wings overhead.

They looked up to see Chad wheeling

above them in the blue sky.

'Mantora and her army have fled,' he called. 'Yerik and his sharks were too much for them. None of our friends were badly hurt, and they are returning to their homes. And you must race straight ahead to your home in Coral Kingdom.'

'Can you help us one more time, Chad?' Lucy asked quickly. 'This Human boy is a friend of ours. How can we get him back to Sandy Bay Island?'

Chad swooped down and settled on the prow of the little boat. 'Perhaps he could swim home with the dolphins who were fighting alongside us,' he said, tipping his head on one side to see Jack better. 'They'll look after him.'

'Swim with the dolphins!' cried Jack. 'That would be wonderful. Thank you so much.' He leaned over the side of the boat and looked solemnly into Lucy's eyes. 'This has been the most magical thing that ever happened to me. I'll never forget you.'

'Forget!' exclaimed Misty. 'Haven't we forgotten something? We're supposed to put a Forgetting Charm on him!'

Chapter Five

The mermaids held hands and formed a circle in the water around the boat, ready to start singing the Forgetting Charm. But Lucy suddenly dropped her hands and said, 'I don't think we should do this.'

The others looked at her in amazement. Quiet, shy Lucy had been so bold today! They had never seen her look quite so determined.

'Why not, Lucy?' asked Holly. 'You know it's one of the Merfolk's Laws. All Humans who accidentally meet any mermaids have to be made to forget all about it.'

'I know,' said Lucy, 'But Jack is different. He doesn't want to harm us, or catch us.'

'Even if we can trust Jack,' said Ellie, 'we can't break the Merfolk Law.'

'Why not?' replied Lucy stubbornly. 'The Law was made to protect us, not imprison us. I've always been timid and afraid. This adventure has taught me that it's sometimes good to take a risk. Even Queen Neptuna did that when she sent us young mermaids to collect the Crystals.'

'That's true,' said Sophie, looking round at the others hovering in the water.

'I think we should take a risk on Jack,' Lucy continued. 'If he remembers us, it will inspire him to look after the sea himself one day, like he said. And he can ask the other Human children to care for the sea creatures that we love.'

'Then so be it,' said Holly. 'But we must be a secret, Jack.'

'I won't tell anyone else,' he promised. 'Not even Dad.'

Lucy quickly searched in her SOS Kit and found her pearly Mermaid Comb. She pushed it into Jack's hands.

'Then farewell,' said the mermaids

kindly. 'Don't forget us.'

Then Lucy turned to look at the sun. It had started to climb down the afternoon sky, slipping closer and closer to its bed in the sea.

'The sunset isn't very far away,' she cried. 'We must go!'

The mermaids had outwitted Mantora's army and rescued Jack. Now they had to put all their energy into racing home with the Crystals.

'*Mermaid SOS!*' they cried, for one last time. The brave young Crystal Keepers dived under the waves. Then they streamed away towards Coral Kingdom, on and on through the last precious hours of the day.

The friends passed silver shoals of mackerel, squirming squid and clouds of tiny shrimps, as they raced though the glimmering sea. They spotted a grey whale and her calf gliding in the cool depths beneath them. They saw mottled green turtles floating near the sun-drenched surface. Still the mermaids swam on without daring to stop, or speak, or rest.

Just when Lucy thought she couldn't move her arms and tail one more time, she saw the beautiful reef that marked the entrance to Coral Kingdom. They were nearly home!

Above the sea, the sun was sinking down in a fiery glow. As Lucy and her friends swooped over the reef, the gleaming towers and turrets of Queen Neptuna's Palace shone below them in the crystal-clear water.

With a sudden swirl of their tails, the mermaids stopped in front of the arching mother-of-pearl gates, which led into the Palace courtyard. All six of them knocked eagerly and called out, 'Let us in! Tell Queen Neptuna that the Sisters of the Sea have returned.'

The gates were flung open. A guard with a bronze helmet and a long spear blew a conch shell like a royal trumpet. Merfolk with worried faces darted forward from all sides of the courtyard.

'We've made it,' called Sophie, 'we've come home.'

Surprised cries broke out around them. 'The young ones are here! Have they got the Crystals? How long is left before sunset?'

'Where is Queen Neptuna?' asked Holly urgently.

On the far side of the underwater garden, the guard opened a tall, carved door and Queen Neptuna herself swam out to greet them.

'We have been worried about you, my dear young ones,' she

exclaimed. 'I am so glad that you are safe.'

'We have done as you asked, Your Majesty,' said Misty quickly. 'We have brought you the new Crystals.'

A huge shout of relief burst out from the anxious Merfolk gathered all around.

'What great news you bring,' proclaimed the Queen, in her rich, clear voice. 'Quickly, everyone, come to the Crystal Throne. The sun is nearly setting!'

Everyone swam eagerly after the Queen into the great hall at the heart of the magnificent Palace. In the centre of the glittering chamber, there stood the ancient Throne, wrought of silver and pearls. Around its edge were the six sparkling Crystals that gave power to the Merfolk.

But these old, dying Crystals no longer
sparkled. They barely gleamed with the
faintest of lights. In a few minutes they
would fade for ever. The Merfolk gathered
round and watched nervously, hardly
bearing to look. At any moment the old
Crystals might flicker out, and Mantora
would triumph. All Coral Kingdom's
hopes rested on the young mermaids,

returned at last from their long journey.

Queen Neptuna swiftly curled her silver tail and sat on the Throne. Her long golden hair flowed over her shoulders and reached down to her waist.

'You have been faithful Crystal Keepers,' she said to the young mermaids. 'You must place the new Crystals in the Throne.'

'You go first, Scarlett,' whispered Misty. 'You deserve it.'

Scarlett gave Misty a quick smile and glided towards the Throne. She held her Crystal in the palm of her hand.

'The first Crystal is to protect the Fish and the Sea Creatures,' said Scarlett. Then she touched one of the old Crystals with her new one. All the Merfolk gasped.

Scarlett's Crystal flew out of her hand. The old and new Crystals spun round together, shooting radiant sparks all around. Then there was a blinding flash of light. When the Merfolk looked again, there was no sign of the old, fading Crystal. In its place, sealed firmly in the silver Throne, was

Scarlett's Crystal. It shone with brilliant new life.

'Now you must all do the same,' urged Queen Neptuna. One by one, the other mermaids touched the old Crystals with the new ones.

'The second Crystal is to protect the Whales and Dolphins,' said Sophie.

'The third Crystal is to protect the Sea Birds,' said Ellie.

'The fourth Crystal is to protect the Sea Plants,' said Holly.

'The fifth Crystal is to protect the Merfolk who care for them all,' said Misty.

The Queen bowed her head graciously to each mermaid in turn, as their new Crystals locked themselves by magic into her Throne. Then she looked at Lucy. 'And

you, little one,' she said. 'What have you
brought?'

Lucy held out her pure, gleaming
Crystal.

'The sixth Crystal is to protect the
Humans who come to the sea,' she said

softly. She gently rippled her green tail,
and reached forward to set the last Crystal
next to the others. But as she did so, a
ghastly voice rang out: 'I COMMAND
YOU TO STOP!'

Every head turned to see what was
making the terrible disturbance, then the
Merfolk's frightened whispers echoed round
the underwater chamber.

It was Mantora, and she had one last
cruel trick to play on the mermaids.

Chapter Six

The Sisters of the Sea hovered bravely around Queen Neptuna's Throne like a guard of honour. They were finally about to see their great enemy face to face.

Mantora swam through the petrified Merfolk, until she hovered insolently in front of the Queen. A long tattered cloak streamed from her shoulders. With a quick flourish, her dark veil was thrown back, revealing a face that had once been beautiful, but was now twisted by malice and spite.

'So, you miserable little mermaids have arrived home,' she snarled. 'But I have brought you a surprise!'

A livid green sea serpent slithered out

from under her billowing cloak. Lucy darted forward with a cry: 'Jack!' The boy's limp body was entwined in the sea monster's clinging coils. His eyes were closed and his face was deathly pale. The life was slowly draining out of him.

'So, you recognise your dear Human friend,' Mantora sneered at Lucy. 'I have a bargain for you, my pretty one. Give me that magic Crystal in your hand and I will release the boy. Then you can return him to his family – but Coral Kingdom will be mine!'

Lucy's brain reeled. How could she make such a choice? If she gave the Crystal to Mantora, the evil reign of Storm Kingdom would begin. But if she refused to do as Mantora commanded, Jack's young life would end…Lucy looked helplessly at Queen Neptuna for guidance. But the Mermaid Queen remained motionless on the Throne, silent like a statue, her eyes fixed on her wicked sister. Yet just as Lucy felt she must despair, Neptuna's clear voice seemed to echo in her head: 'Strength and courage, Lucy. Believe in the Magic!'

The young mermaid looked down at the Crystal that she was still clasping in her hand. Deep in the heart of it, a green fire seemed to burn. Lucy didn't feel shy or nervous any more. Without thinking, she lifted her Crystal and thrust it into Mantora's eyes. A great flame of light burst from the glittering stone.

'Aaayeee!' screeched Mantora, clutching her dazzled eyes. 'You have blinded me!'

She and her sea serpent writhed on the
rocky floor of the chamber, their scaly tails
tangled in a snaky heap. Lucy shot
forward and grabbed hold of Jack's lifeless
body. She flicked her tail with all her
might, and set off for the surface, dragging
the boy with her. Misty, Ellie, Sophie,
Holly and Scarlett rushed to help. Soon

they were all racing up, up, up, getting closer to the Overwater world where Jack belonged. With a great splash, they burst through the waves.

Chad was hovering anxiously near the empty green boat, surrounded by a pod of sleek dolphins.

'Mantora and her sea serpents sneaked back and ambushed us, when we were setting off with Jack,' he called. 'But you have rescued him just in time!'

The mermaids managed to heave the boy into the boat. He lay still for a moment, blinking in the rosy evening light. Lucy gently passed her Crystal over his mouth and heart. Then he coughed and choked and started to breathe once more.

'The dolphins will guide the boat back

to Sandy Bay Island with their strong beaks,' said Chad. 'We will guard them. Nothing will stop us getting your friend home safely this time.'

Jack opened his eyes and looked at Lucy and the other mermaids, as they clustered around the boat.

'You've saved my life...' he whispered. 'I'll never forget you...but the sun is setting...now go and save Coral Kingdom!'

Lucy smiled at him, then leaped up in a shining arc before diving into the water. The huge red sun was just about to slip below the horizon. Lucy knew what she must do, and she felt brave and strong. Followed by her friends, she swam faster than she had ever swum before, straight back to the royal chamber where Queen Neptuna was waiting. Lucy swirled to a stop at the silver Throne.

'The last Crystal is to protect our Human friends,' she cried. Then she reached out and touched the old Crystal, as its very last ray of light flickered and faded. The sixth new Crystal spun into its place in a shower of sparks. The Throne shone like a glittering star. At last, the Mermaid Magic was complete.

'Hooray for Coral Kingdom,' shouted the Merfolk. 'Hooray for the young mermaids! Lucy! Misty! Ellie! Sophie! Holly! Scarlett! Praise them!'

Lucy and her friends blushed and smiled, their eyes sparkling with joy. Queen

Neptuna looked more beautiful than ever. Her pale skin glowed as though bathed in moonlight, and her hair glinted like pure gold. She and her Kingdom were full of new, radiant power. The walls of the underwater cavern glimmered with mother-of-pearl. Coloured light poured from the Throne over the Merfolk, like a living fountain of diamonds, rubies, sapphires, emeralds and amethysts.

But then Mantora slowly swam up from the floor, angrily rubbing her bloodshot eyes. She was weakened, though not totally conquered.

'Don't forget,' she rasped, 'the new Crystals will only last for one more year. I'll defeat you next time!'

'But why should you wish to defeat me,

my sister?' Queen Neptuna stretched out her hand. 'Come, I will share my kingdom with you, if only you will return to our Merfolk family.'

'Never,' spat Mantora. 'If I can't have Coral Kingdom for myself alone, I'd rather see the whole sea destroyed.'

'Then I am sorry for you,' sighed the Queen.

'Don't waste your pity,' replied Mantora. 'I'll be back!' With a bitter curse, she and her sea serpent twisted away in a fierce flurry of bubbles, making everyone shudder as they swam past.

'Do not be afraid, my good Merfolk,' said Queen Neptuna, raising her hand for quiet. 'We will not be crushed by her empty threats. She cannot return now the Crystals are renewed. Coral Kingdom is safe, thanks to our young mermaids. Let us rejoice!'

Cheers rang out on every side. The six happy mermaids hugged each other joyfully. Then Queen Neptuna beckoned them to her side.

'So, my brave ones,' she said, 'I have learned that I was right to trust you with this task. And what did you learn from your adventure?'

The mermaids looked at each other. They had done and seen so many things. Memories of crabs and cuttlefish, dolphins and turtles, seals, sharks and soaring sea birds rushed into their minds in a confused parade. But at last, Lucy spoke up.

'I think, Your Majesty,' she said quietly, 'that however many lessons we have learned, there is one thing that we will never forget.'

'And what is that, my child?'

'That we're willing to do anything, and go

anywhere, and learn anything, if it will make us better Sisters of the Sea,' replied Lucy. The others murmured happily in agreement.

'Then you have all learned much,' smiled the Queen. 'And I may need to ask my young mermaids to help me again soon. But life is not all tasks and lessons. Now it is time to celebrate. Here are your families to welcome you home.'

Home! They really were home at last. Lucy, Misty, Ellie, Sophie, Holly and Scarlett threw themselves gladly into the arms of their families. There was Lucy's mother with tears in her eyes, and Scarlett's proud father, Holly's beaming brothers, and Misty's little sister Dusty, looking as though she would burst with happiness. On all sides, the dearest mothers and fathers in the world were eager to hug and kiss their beloved mermaid daughters.

The Crystals burned brightly in Queen Neptuna's Throne once more. And in the young mermaids' hearts, there burned a flame of friendship, that would never, ever fade.

THE END

.......Or is it?

Mermaid Sisters of the Sea

Misty has flowing blonde hair and a shimmering pink tail. Misty is a really determined and brave mermaid.

Ellie is very caring and loves sea birds. She has long, wavy dark hair and a glittering purple tail.

Sophie has funky fair hair and a blazing, bright orange tail, which helps her to swim super fast.

Holly has sweet, short black hair and a dazzling yellow tail. Holly is very thoughtful and clever.

Scarlett has fabulous, thick dark hair and a gleaming red tail. She can be a little bit bossy and headstrong sometimes.

Lucy has fiery red hair and an emerald green tail, but don't let that fool you – she is really quite shy.

By the same author

Mermaid S.O.S
Misty to the Rescue
gillian shields

Mermaid S.O.S
Ellie and the Secret Potion
gillian shields

Mermaid S.O.S
Sophie Makes a Splash
gillian shields

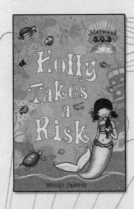

Mermaid S.O.S
Holly Takes a Risk
gillian shields

Mermaid S.O.S
Scarlett's New Friend
gillian shields

Mermaid S.O.S
Lucy and the Magic Crystal
gillian shields

To order from Bookpost PO Box 29 Douglas Isle of Man IM99 1BQ www.bookpost.co.uk
email: bookshop@enterprise.net fax: 01624 837033 tel: 01624 836000

www.bloomsbury.com